A Strange Case of
MAGIC

Other books by Kenneth Oppel

Barnes and the Brains Series:
    A Bad Case of Ghosts
    A Strange Case of Magic
    *A Crazy Case of Robots**
    *An Incredible Case of Dinosaurs**
    *A Weird Case of Super-Goo**
Emma's Emu
Silverwing
Sunwing
The Live-Forever Machine
Dead Water Zone
Peg and the Whale
Follow that Star

                    * forthcoming

A Strange Case of MAGIC

KENNETH OPPEL

Illustrated by
Sam Sisco

Scholastic Canada Ltd.

Scholastic Canada Ltd.
175 Hillmount Rd., Markham, Ontario, Canada L6C 1Z7

Scholastic Inc.
555 Broadway, New York, NY 10012, USA

Scholastic Australia Pty Limited
PO Box 579, Gosford, NSW 2250, Australia

Scholastic New Zealand Ltd.
Private Bag 94407, Greenmount, Auckland,
New Zealand

Scholastic Publications Ltd.
Villiers House, Clarendon Avenue, Leamington Spa,
Warwickshire CV32 5PR, UK

Canadian Cataloguing in Publication Data

Oppel, Kenneth
  A strange case of magic

(Barnes and the brains)
ISBN 0-439-98732-6

I. Title. II. Series: Oppel, Kenneth. Barnes and the brains.

PS8579.P64S77 2000   jC813'.54   C00-930781-8
PZ7.O66St 2000

6 5 4 3 2 1   Printed in Canada   0 1 2 3 4 5/0

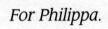

For Philippa.

Contents

Chapter 1

Allergic to Books

GILES BARNES LOOKED at his watch.

Tina and Kevin were late. They were almost never late, especially not for the library. Giles liked the old library. He liked the big, bright reading room with its tall, arched windows and varnished floors. He liked the sounds of the library, too: paper softly rustling, people mumbling, and Miss Hibbins snoring at her desk.

"Miss Hibbins," Giles whispered, gently touching her arm.

"Oh, hello!" she said, snapping upright. "Was I asleep?"

Giles nodded.

"I try my best, Giles, I really do, but this place is

just so totally boring . . ."

"Miss Hibbins, you're the librarian."

"I know. There's no escape for me. But what's your excuse?"

"I'm waiting for Tina and Kevin."

Miss Hibbins looked impressed. "Oh, you mean the Quark geniuses!"

"That's right," said Giles.

"You're keeping good company, I've got to hand it to you. But I thought they only spoke to geniuses. Are you a genius, Giles?"

"Well, they made me an honorary member," Giles replied awkwardly. "But I don't think I'm really genius material."

"Well, so few are," said Miss Hibbins sympathetically. "Tina fixed my television once, you know. Charged me an arm and a leg for it, but it hasn't given me any trouble since. She's got a mind like a photocopier."

"She's very smart," said Giles, a little enviously.

It wasn't easy having friends who were geniuses. Tina and Kevin Quark were always inventing things, amazing gadgets that beeped and hummed and shot out smoke and sparks. Tina could multiply faster than a calculator, and

2

she could figure out the exact number of jaw-breakers in a big glass jar, just by glancing at it. She could even understand the instructions for do-it-yourself furniture. She was definitely a genius.

Just then the library doors swung open and Tina Quark strode in. She was very tiny, with two precise blond braids hanging on either side of her head. In one small hand, she held a paperback. Behind her staggered Kevin, loaded down with a stack of books so high he could barely see where he was going. Only a few strands of his curly red hair could be seen, poking up above the tower of textbooks. Several paperbacks were jammed under his armpits as well. He teetered into the reading room after his sister.

"Um, Tina — " he began to say.

"We're almost there, Kevin."

Kevin staggered to the right, then to the left, the stack of books swaying crazily from side to side.

"I think I'm going to — "

But it was too late. Kevin gave a mighty sneeze and the huge tower of books came crashing to the ground.

"Oh, excellent work, Kevin!" said Tina in exasperation.

"I told you, I'm allergic to books!" Kevin exclaimed.

"You are not allergic to books," his sister said sternly.

"Well, I don't see why I had to carry them all in the first place!"

Giles walked over to help Kevin pick up the books.

"Hello, Barnes," Tina said. "Sorry we're late. As you can see, Kevin had some trouble with the relatively simple task of walking."

"You try carrying twenty books at the same time!" Kevin muttered indignantly.

"It's a question of balance and momentum," said Tina wisely. "You didn't take that into account, did you?"

"No, I suppose not."

"Well, you'll know next time. Hello, Miss Hibbins. We'd like to return a few books."

"They were pretty boring," Kevin whispered to Giles as they lugged the books over to the counter. "Hardly any pictures."

"Kevin," said Tina, "please don't forget, even

for one second, that you have a very tiny brain."

"You see," Kevin said to Giles long-sufferingly, "you see what I have to put up with?"

"What are we looking for today, Tina?" Giles asked.

"I need a few more books for my latest invention," she said.

"What exactly is the latest invention?" Giles inquired.

"I'm afraid I can't tell you that just now."

"Why not?"

"It's not finished yet."

Giles rolled his eyes.

"Don't worry," Kevin told him. "She doesn't even tell me, and I'm her brother — and a fellow genius as well." He sneaked a wary glance at Tina to see if she would object.

"Well then," she said briskly, "let's not waste another second. To the book stacks!"

Chapter 2

Magic Books

THE STAIRS LEADING down to the book stacks were narrow and dimly lit. Giles liked going down them; he felt secret and mysterious, like an archaeologist exploring an underground tomb. He walked amongst the tall shelves, trying to match the numbers on the book spines with the numbers Tina had scribbled out for him. His feet clanged along the metal catwalks. When he looked down, he could see the tops of people's heads on the floor below. In the distance, he heard the faint echo of Tina and Kevin's voices.

After a few minutes he found one of Tina's books, high on a shelf. He pulled over a small step ladder, climbed up, and yanked out the book.

From his high vantage point, he could see over the tops of the stacks in front of him.

Something caught his eye. He squinted. A book had slid out from one of the shelves and was floating in thin air. Giles gaped. He scrubbed his eyes with his fists to make sure he was seeing right.

The book opened by itself, and all the pages fluttered, as if some ghostly hand were riffling through them.

Giles took a deep breath. Another book glided out from the shelf and stacked itself on top of the first. Slowly, Giles stepped down from the ladder. He tiptoed around the stacks, and soon found Tina and Kevin.

"There's something I think you should see," he whispered.

"I don't think so, Barnes. I'm quite occupied right now."

"No. Really. You'll want to see this."

"Why?"

"You'd better take a look for yourself," Giles said. He held a finger to his lips, and led them stealthily back to where he'd seen the floating books. All three poked their heads carefully around the corner.

Kevin's eyes widened in amazement, but Tina looked very calm.

A tower of six or seven books swayed in mid-air.

"Fascinating," Tina mumbled to herself.

"Um, Tina — " Kevin said in a whisper.

"Not now," Tina said.

"Na-na-na-*chooo*!"

Giles jumped, Tina jumped, even the floating books seemed to give a jump. Then the books started moving through the air, down the corridor. Giles thought he heard the sound of footsteps ringing out against the metal floor, but they quickly faded away.

Tina gave her brother a withering look. "You picked an interesting moment to sneeze."

"It's all these books," Kevin said sheepishly. "What can I do?"

"I only wish I'd had longer to make observations," said his sister.

Giles cautiously moved closer to the large gap in the shelf.

"They were all books on magic tricks," said Tina simply.

Giles glanced over at her in surprise. "How'd you know?"

"Barnes," Tina began, "I don't think it would be an exaggeration for me to say I've read most of the books in this library." She waved her hand at the gap on the shelf. "This section here, for instance, is where the books on magic are kept. I recognize the shelf numbers."

"And now they're all gone," mumbled Kevin, shaking his head.

"It was like the books were being pulled out and stacked up by someone," Giles said. "Or something!"

"Ghosts!" said Kevin.

"Most possibly," said Tina. "I think we should have a chat with Miss Hibbins."

Chapter 3

A Ghost in the Library?

"I JUST SAW a tower of books float out the main doors," said Miss Hibbins, mopping her forehead with a section of newspaper. The newsprint smudged off on her moist forehead, so that Giles could read the day's headlines.

He patted her reassuringly on the arm. "We saw the same thing," he said.

"I've never known anything like it," the librarian continued. Her eyes had an unusual shine to them. "Just straight out the door, *whoosh.*"

"Miss Hibbins," Tina began solemnly, "are you

aware of any ghostly disturbances in this library?"

Miss Hibbins's eyes widened, and her mouth wobbled around a bit, searching for words.

"Well . . . I . . . no! I mean, there was Roger, years ago, but he wasn't a ghost, though people thought he was fairly odd. I mean, he was awfully pale, but — "

"Miss Hibbins," interrupted Giles gently, "you might have a ghost in your library."

The librarian looked nervously around the room, making sure no one was listening.

"Here?" she said in a whisper.

"Someone, or something, just took out all the books on magic," Giles told her.

"And they weren't even signed out," said Miss Hibbins, sounding genuinely annoyed. "Completely against the rules."

"Ghosts get away with an awful lot," said Kevin, nodding wisely.

"You really think there's a ghost in the library?" Miss Hibbins asked again.

"Nothing has been proven," Tina said firmly. "But we'd like to carry out some tests. We'll need the ghostometer."

"The ghostometer?" said Miss Hibbins.

"A personal invention of mine," Tina told her briskly. "It measures ghost activity. It's been highly successful in the past."

"I see," said Miss Hibbins. "Well, I think that's a good idea. I mean, nobody wants some inconsiderate ghoul roaming around the stacks."

"He'd scare the heck out of everyone," Giles agreed.

"Oh, I'm not worried about that!" Miss Hibbins exclaimed. "I'm worried about the books! I don't want some greedy ghost gobbling up all my books!"

"Um, we'll do our best," said Giles.

"Still," said the librarian, getting into the spirit of things, "it does liven the place up a bit, doesn't it?"

"I think," said Tina, looking at Miss Hibbins, "it would be best not to mention this to anyone until we've investigated further."

"Oh, of course!" whispered Miss Hibbins with the utmost secrecy. "Whatever you say!"

Chapter 4

In the Workshop

"WELL," SAID MR. BARNES, "it's just as well your mother's not home to hear any of this."

"I know," said Giles. "She's not a big fan of ghosts."

Giles's mother was a professor of mathematics at the university, and fortunately, she was away at a conference for several days. Mrs. Barnes believed in long numbers and decimal points. She believed in fractions and equals signs. She did not believe in ghosts. But a few months ago, she had enjoyed the mind-opening experience of having her house haunted by ghost birds. After that, she'd grudgingly had to change her mind. Luckily, Giles, with Tina and Kevin's help, had managed to get rid of the ghost birds before Mrs. Barnes went insane.

"It's amazing where they pop up, isn't it," said Mr. Barnes, shaking his head in wonderment. "The library, of all places! And magic books! What would a ghost want with magic books? Could you pass me that saw, please?"

Mr. Barnes was building a set of bookshelves in the garage, and Giles watched with admiration as his father sawed a thick piece of wood in a perfect straight line. Whenever Giles tried, the line went all wobbly, or the saw blade got stuck halfway through. He liked building models and gluing things together, especially airplanes, but when it came to woodworking, he felt clumsy.

"Tina wants to do some tests tomorrow with the ghostometer," Giles said.

"Ah yes, the great ghostometer," said Mr. Barnes, smiling. "She's very good at those inventions of hers."

Giles nodded ruefully, wondering what *he* was very good at.

"Dad," he asked, "do you think Tina's really a genius?"

Mr. Barnes looked at his son curiously. "Well,

she's certainly very confident, isn't she. But if you want my real opinion, Giles, I think she's a little too confident. Don't forget about all those disasters of hers."

Giles nodded gratefully. He hadn't forgotten. Mr. and Mrs. Quark were often shutting down Tina and Kevin's genius business when things got out of hand — when strange and alarming smells wafted up from their basement workshop, or when too many kitchen appliances mysteriously vanished, or when potted plants suddenly started growing out of control.

Mr. Barnes smiled at his son. "You be careful tomorrow," he said.

"Of course," said Giles, but he knew that even though ghosts might be frightening, they couldn't harm anyone in the real world.

"You know something," said Giles. "I don't think it's a ghost at all."

"Really?" said Mr. Barnes, surprised. "Why's that?"

Giles knew he couldn't explain. It was just a feeling he had. For one thing, would ghosts take out library books? Would they make footsteps? Maybe, or maybe not. Or maybe he hadn't really

17

heard footsteps at all — it was just his imagination.

"It just didn't feel like a ghost," Giles told his father, and that was all he could say.

Chapter 5

The Disappearing Act

NEXT MORNING, Giles met Tina and Kevin at the library. It was a Saturday and there was hardly anyone inside. Kevin had tissues jutting out of all his pockets and occasionally would yank one out and give his nose a big blast. Tina carried the ghostometer around her neck on a thick strap. It looked like a large toaster with various switches and buttons added on.

Miss Hibbins eyed the gadget in wonder. "You invented that all by yourself?" she asked Tina.

"That's correct, yes."

"Incredible! You must be the youngest, most brilliant inventor of all time!"

"You may very well be right," said Tina, smiling faintly.

"Please. Don't encourage her," Giles whispered to the librarian. "You'll only make her worse."

"Shall we proceed?" Tina said in her most professional voice. "Miss Hibbins, it would be most helpful if you would remain behind, and discourage people from going downstairs until we're finished."

"Sure," said Miss Hibbins, beaming, obviously pleased to have a role, no matter how small, in the goings-on.

Down in the book stacks, Tina pulled a large set of headphones over her ears and twiddled with the ghostometer.

"The ghost should have left strong traces," Tina said. "I am now going to take some readings."

Giles waited impatiently as Tina walked up and down the rows of shelves, concentrating intently. He couldn't shake the feeling that what they'd seen yesterday wasn't a ghost at all. But he couldn't tell Tina that. She would just shake her head and say he was unscientific. That's what happened when you had friends who were geniuses.

"This is extremely odd," Tina whispered after a few moments. "I'm not picking up anything at all. Not even a single beep."

"What about a blerp?" Kevin asked. "Any blerps?"

Tina sighed. "No, Kevin. No blerps either."

"That's bad," said Kevin. "When there aren't any blerps — "

"Shhh!" said Giles.

Through a gap in the shelves, he could see a tower of books floating down the corridor towards them. He dived out of sight behind a nearby trolley, and the Quarks hurried after him.

"Now remember, Kevin," whispered Tina, "you sneeze again, and I'm asking Mom and Dad to put you up for adoption."

The ghostly stack of books glided around the corner and hovered for a moment. Then, one by one, the books began to slide back into their proper place on the shelf.

If it was a ghost doing this, Giles thought to himself, at least it was a very considerate one. Miss Hibbins would approve.

He glanced at Tina. She was pressing the head-phones tight against her head and frowning in confusion. Giles couldn't bear the wait any longer. He yanked the headphones off Tina's ears and clamped them over his own.

There was nothing to be heard. Not a beep, not a blerp, not so much as a ghostly whimper!

"There must be something wrong with the ghostometer," Tina said, mouthing the words to Giles.

"Or else it's not a ghost at all," Giles said, mouthing the words back.

The last book had mysteriously glided back into place on the shelf and Giles's eyes roved intently through the air, searching for some kind of ghostly shimmer. But he saw nothing.

"It's hopeless," said a man's quiet voice, "absolutely hopeless."

Giles could feel the hair on his forearms tingle with electricity.

"Who's there?" he demanded, his voice trembling a little.

"Nobody!" came the startled reply.

"It's a ghost!" said Kevin.

"Are you a ghost?" Tina asked in a calm voice.

"No," came the mournful reply. "I'm not a ghost. I'm just . . . invisible."

"Why are you invisible?" Giles asked, peering out from around the trolley.

"It's magic," said the man. "A very bad case of magic."

"Someone made you invisible?" Giles asked.

"It's too humiliating," said the man. "I was hoping no one would ever have to know. But what's the use trying to hide it now. I made myself invisible. I'm a magician."

"A magician!" said Kevin, beaming. "Wow! I've never met a magician before!"

"Well, the thing is, I'm not a very good magician," the man went on. "I'm really more of an apprentice."

"Oh, you're just learning," Kevin said.

"Kevin," said Tina with a sigh, "that's what apprentice *means*."

"Sorry."

"So you made yourself invisible on purpose?" Giles inquired, still confused.

"It's not a happy story," said the mournful magician. "I was doing a small magic show at a birthday party. It was actually my first magic show ever. And they were tough, those kids. They were not easily impressed. They got impatient. They hooted. They hollered. I began to make mistakes! I tried to pull a rabbit out of my hat, but I got a cucumber instead! It was all downhill from there."

Giles waited for the invisible magician to continue.

"Well, I thought I would try one last trick. I wasn't even planning on it, but what choice did I have? I had to do something pretty spectacular or I was finished! I tried the Disappearing Act! It worked!"

"You must have been pleased," said Kevin.

"Oh, I was — for about thirty seconds!" said the invisible magician. "Then I discovered I couldn't make myself come back. So here I am . . . or here I'm not. It all gets a little confusing when you're invisible! My name's Vikram Kapoor, by the way."

"I'm Giles Barnes," said Giles. Without thinking, he extended his hand, and immediately felt foolish. But before he could jam his hand back into his pocket, he felt the grip of cool, invisible fingers around his. His whole body went tingly, and he watched in amazement as his arm pumped up and down in the air. He was getting an invisible hand-shake.

"I'm pleased to meet you, Barnes," said the

magician. "I'm pleased to meet all of you. It's terribly lonely being invisible."

"Is this why you've been taking out the magic books?" said Giles. "To figure out how to come back?"

"Yes. But none of the spells seem to work."

"We can help you out!" Kevin blurted enthusiastically. "We're geniuses!"

Tina shot her brother an incinerating glare. "Mr. Kapoor," she said, "you may not have heard of us, but we operate a small business specializing in just about everything. Kevin, give him one of our cards."

Kevin rummaged through his trouser pockets and produced a dog-eared rectangle of paper. He blew the dust off and held it out into the air, where it gently drifted away from his fingers.

"Ah," said Mr. Kapoor, reading the business card. "You're local geniuses, I see."

"That's right. Mr. Kapoor, let me be frank. I'd be very interested in taking on your case. It just so happens that I myself have been experimenting with an energy ray that might very well solve your invisibility problem."

"So that's what we've been working on!" Kevin

said. "An energy ray!" He looked at Giles, shaking his head. "She doesn't tell me anything."

"You really think you could cure my invisibility?" Mr. Kapoor said excitedly.

"I can't promise anything right now," Tina said, "but based on our numerous successes in the past, I think it's highly likely."

"Well, this is fantastic!" said the invisible magician.

"Shall we meet back here in a few days?" Tina said. "I want to get to work immediately."

Chapter 6

The Energy Ray

"I'VE ALWAYS WANTED to learn magic," said Giles.

"So have I," said Kevin.

"No you haven't," said Tina, rummaging around in her toolbox.

"I have," Kevin insisted hotly. "You don't know everything about me! I've often considered becoming a magician!"

"Kevin, remember what I said about your brain," Tina reminded him.

"I know, I know," Kevin grumbled. "Very tiny."

"Very, *very* tiny."

Giles shook his head. Tina was being awfully hard on Kevin lately. She was already at work on her energy ray in the Quarks' basement workshop. Giles sat beside Kevin on a wooden crate, turning through the pages of one of the magic books they'd brought home from the library.

"This is a good one," he said to Kevin. "It has all kinds of lessons for beginners."

"It's all junk," said Tina disdainfully, plugging in her soldering iron, "all trickery and sleight of hand. It's completely unscientific. Don't you think you're wasting your time?"

"No," said Giles, "I don't. If we know more about it, maybe we'll be able to help Mr. Kapoor better."

"Let me take care of that," said Tina, melting globs of lead onto electrical wires.

Giles inspected the large machine on Tina's workbench.

"It looks like a film projector," he said.

"It used to *be* a film projector," Kevin pointed out, "before Tina got her hands on it. What if Mom and Dad want to watch some home movies?"

"Spare me," said Tina. "I think this is a bit more important, don't you? Besides, I've been telling them to buy a video camera for ages. They're so old-fashioned."

Kevin grunted. He was reading the magic book again. "Hey, I think I can do this one." He reached for the deck of cards. "Let's give it a try. Pick a card, Barnes. Any card."

Giles picked a card.

"Um, maybe not that one," said Kevin, glancing back down at the instructions in the book. "Here, try . . . this one."

Smiling, Giles took the card Kevin handed him.

"All right!" said Kevin, "Here we go!"

He reshuffled the deck of cards, divided them into several piles, swirled them round on the table, piled them up again, glanced at a few of the cards, shuffled them for a second and then a third time, tapped them with his knuckles, then pressed his fingers to his temples.

"Barnes," he said, "the card you chose was the ace of spades."

Giles checked his card. "No."

"No?"

Kevin collected up all his cards and began rifling through them. "All right, what about the three of diamonds."

"Wrong again."

Tina looked up from her gadget with a sigh.

"This is very sad to see, you two. You can't actually believe this is going to help us."

"The twelve of diamonds!" Kevin exclaimed.

"Kevin," said Giles, "there's no such thing as a twelve of diamonds."

"Your card is the four of clubs, Barnes," Tina said.

"How did you know?" Giles demanded.

"I looked at your card," Tina replied. "It's the simplest, and therefore most logical, method."

"Well, this isn't real magic anyway," said Kevin huffily. "This is just beginner's stuff. I need something more challenging."

"Put the cards away," Tina instructed. "It's now time to test the energy ray. Kevin, go stand over there." She waved her hand imperiously to the other side of the room.

"What for?" Kevin asked, wary.

"We need to test the energy ray."

"Not on me!" said Kevin.

"Maybe you should test it on something else first," Giles suggested. "Something that isn't alive."

"Use my shoe," Kevin said, wrenching off one of his red sneakers and placing it on top of a crate.

"All right," Tina sighed. "Stand back, everyone."

She flipped a switch. The machine rattled and hummed for a few moments before sending out a narrow beam of light. The beam hit Kevin's sneaker. It glowed brightly for a moment and then vanished.

"Amazing!" gasped Kevin.

"I think that was a success," said Tina primly.

"Can you get it back?" Giles asked. He was impressed, too, but he'd learned from experience that Tina's inventions didn't always do what they were supposed to.

"Of course," said the tiny girl. "It's a simple matter of reversing the ray's energy." She twiddled with the machine for a few seconds. "Watch."

The ray of light shot out again. Slowly, an object began to appear on top of the crate. It was certainly a shoe, but it was definitely not the same shoe Kevin had taken off his foot. This shoe was black, and about half the size of the original. The shoelaces looked singed, and smoke was curling up from the rubber soles.

"Oh dear," said Tina. "Something seems to be a little off."

"A little *off!*" Kevin cried. "That could have been me!"

"I don't think it's quite ready yet," Giles said. "It's not safe for people."

"That was my best pair of sneakers," Kevin muttered, gingerly picking up his smouldering shoe.

Chapter 7

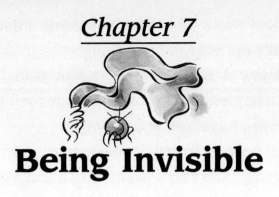

Being Invisible

"IT'S NOT EASY being invisible," said Vikram Kapoor the next day in the library. "The bus won't stop for you. It's impossible to get service in stores, and just try walking down the street without someone bumping into you! Invisible people don't have any rights!"

"It must be really hard," Giles said. "I'm sorry we don't have better news for you. But the energy ray isn't ready yet."

"I'm sure it's a simple matter of minor readjustments," Tina added.

"Well, I'm very grateful for all your help," said the invisible magician. "I spent most of yesterday trying to make myself reappear, but it's just not working. I was a fool to try to become a magician. I'm really not very good at things."

"I know how you feel," Kevin said. "I'm a genius, but my sister's an even bigger genius. Sometimes it can get you down."

"I've been learning some magic tricks," said Giles shyly. "And I was wondering if you'd give me a few tips on the billiard ball trick."

"Why ask me?" said the magician sadly. "I'm hopeless."

"I bet you could show me how," said Giles. "Look, I brought all the stuff."

From his knapsack he produced a bright red billiard ball, a small wooden box, and a large silk handkerchief. His Aunt Lillian, years ago, had given him a magic kit for his birthday, and he had recently rummaged through the closet for it.

"Well . . ." said Mr. Kapoor.

"Please," said Giles.

"All right. I was pretty good at this one, actually. Now let me see."

The magician's invisible hands lifted the red ball and handkerchief into the air, holding them out for everyone to see. Then he swirled the handkerchief dramatically around the ball, wrapping it out of sight.

"Observe, now, as I put the ball into the box."

Giles watched attentively as Mr. Kapoor opened the box and placed the ball inside. He then shut the lid and handed it to Tina.

"You may now open the box," he said.

Tina rattled the box suspiciously, checking to make sure the ball was inside. She opened the lid, and grabbed hold of the handkerchief. But there was no billiard ball to be seen.

"Amazing!" said Kevin. "Where is it?"

"It's in the box, where I put it," said Mr. Kapoor. He picked up the box and lifted out the ball.

"There's obviously some elementary trick to this," grumbled Tina.

"No tricks," said Mr. Kapoor. "Only magic. Now I'll show you, Barnes."

With Mr. Kapoor's invisible hands guiding his, Giles went through the trick. His hands felt graceful and deft; he could feel the magic of the trick flowing from Mr. Kapoor into his own fingers, and then into the billiard ball, the handkerchief, and the wooden box.

For the second time, Tina opened the box and found the ball missing. And then Giles made it

magically reappear. He couldn't help smiling at the grumpy look on Tina's face.

"Silly tricks," she grumbled. "All of it."

"You're a good teacher!" Giles said to Mr. Kapoor.

"You really think so?" said the invisible magician.

For a moment, Giles was certain he could see a flickering shape in the air. He watched expectantly. It was almost as if Mr. Kapoor was faintly reappearing for a second, but then the shadowy image faded quickly away.

"I'm not a good magician though," said Mr. Kapoor, sounding very sad again. "Tina's right. This is all just silly tricks. It's not going to help bring me back. I'm just not good enough. There's not much time left either. If you stay in the disappearing act for too long, there's a chance you might *really* disappear."

"But that's terrible!" Giles cried. "There's got to be other magic books — other tricks and spells that might help! I'll start looking right away!"

"Don't worry, Mr. Kapoor," said Kevin confidently. "We'll have the energy ray working in no time. After all, we *are* geniuses."

Chapter 8

Magic Tricks

"HEY, YOU'RE GETTING good!" Mr. Barnes said.

Giles smiled. He'd been practising magic tricks in the garage while his father worked on the book-shelves, hammering and sanding. By now Giles had perfected the billiard ball trick, and had polished off several others, too.

"It's all pretty easy stuff," he told his father, making a green handkerchief turn yellow.

"It doesn't look easy," said Mr. Barnes. "I couldn't do it. I wouldn't have the confidence."

Giles couldn't help feeling pleased. For the first time, he felt like he was really good at something. "Well, Tina thinks it's all a waste of time," he said.

"She's not impressed."

"I'm impressed."

"Yeah, but you're my Dad!"

"Can't argue with you there," said Mr. Barnes. "How's Mr. Kapoor doing?"

"I'm really worried about him," Giles said, setting down his magic equipment. "Kevin and I have been looking around for more magic books, but we haven't found anything new. And Miss Hibbins said she'd look, too. But I think we're running out of time."

"What about Tina's energy ray?"

Giles shrugged. "Maybe, if it's working in time. But I've got the feeling it's going to take something more powerful than that to bring back Mr. Kapoor."

"You may be right," said Mr. Barnes. "There's more in heaven and earth than is dreamt of in Tina's philosophy."

"Wow!" said Giles. "What does that mean?"

"It means," said Mr. Barnes, "that Tina might be headed for a few surprises."

Giles looked at his watch and jumped. "I've got to go," he said. "Tina and Kevin are testing the energy ray again."

"Kevin, I don't suppose you'd care to volunteer a part of your body for this test," said Tina. "A leg, or a hand, perhaps?"

"Not a chance!"

"I thought not. Well, I brought another test subject."

Tina opened an old trunk and pulled out a stuffed giraffe. She placed it on the cardboard crate at the far end of the room and then retreated behind the energy ray.

"Let's see how it works now," she said.

The beam of violet light shot out from the machine and the stuffed giraffe immediately disappeared.

"So far so good," said Giles hopefully. "Now bring it back."

Tina fiddled with the machine, then switched it on again. The beam of light shot out, and slowly, the giraffe reappeared. There were no singed bits this time, no smoke, no blackened fur.

The only problem was, the stuffed giraffe was at least twice its original size.

Tina looked at it thoughtfully for a few moments.

"Well," she said, "it's pretty close."

"Absolutely not!" said Giles. "We can't use that thing on Mr. Kapoor! He'd come back the size of a giant!"

"Hmmm," said Tina. "I must say, I think you're being a little picky."

"Look," said Giles firmly. "There's only one way to bring Mr. Kapoor back, and that's the same way he got there! Magic!"

Chapter 9

A New Spell

"I FOUND IT in the basement of the rare book library," said Miss Hibbins excitedly. "It took me hours to track down!"

She handed Giles a thick leather-bound volume. The thin pages crinkled as he turned them. It was an ancient book of magic, written in faded, flowing script and filled with strange diagrams and symbols.

"Thank you very much," said Giles gratefully.

He searched hurriedly through the book until he found what he was looking for. On the very last pages was a description of the Disappearing Act, with instructions on how to reappear at the end.

"This might just do the trick," Giles mumbled. "I

don't think I've seen this one before. Maybe it's powerful enough to bring Mr. Kapoor back!"

"I think we're wasting our time," said Tina.

"You don't know that yet," said Giles firmly.

"It's at least worth a try," piped in Kevin.

Tina glared at him.

"Well, our energy ray's broken, isn't it!"

"Broken is a little harsh, Kevin," said Tina primly. "Unperfected is perhaps a more accurate description."

"I'd just like to say that this is the most thrilling thing that's ever happened to me!" said Miss Hibbins, glowing with excitement.

"Well, I'm glad to hear it," said Giles with a smile. He turned back to Tina and Kevin. "Come on, Mr. Kapoor will be here soon."

Downstairs in the book stacks, they waited for the invisible magician to arrive. Then Giles quickly told him about the spell in the ancient book.

"I doubt it will work," said Mr. Kapoor dolefully. "Nothing seems to work for me."

"First, it is essential you clear your mind of all thoughts," said Giles, reading from the dusty tome.

"All right," came the magician's voice after a

moment. "Now what?"

"Calm your breathing," instructed Giles.

"Yes."

"Make a circle in the air with your right hand, and a triangle with your left."

Tina shook her head sadly, not believing any of it.

"Now, read the rest yourself," Giles said, offering the heavy book to the empty air.

"Waxum. Holvex. Intra Quandum!" murmured Mr. Kapoor, reading from the book's crackling pages. "Javex. Ultrex. Mega Maxum!"

"Keep going!" said Giles.

"Optrex. Apex. Visitixis!"

There was a long silence. Giles watched the air in front of him expectantly, but nothing happened.

"It's not working," said Mr. Kapoor miserably. "I knew it wouldn't. I'm a terrible magician. I can't even follow a recipe!"

"I'm sorry," said Giles, discouraged. "I thought this one would do the trick."

"It's not your fault, Barnes," said Mr. Kapoor. "It's me. I'm just no good at any of it! I was a fool to become a magician!"

Chapter 10

The Plan

GILES SAT IN the Quarks' basement workshop, listlessly watching Kevin try to do a magic trick. He felt discouraged and helpless. Mr. Kapoor was fading away fast, and he couldn't think up any clever ideas that might help.

Beside him, Tina stared at the large, empty space on her workbench.

"I can't believe they confiscated it," she said. "Have they no idea of the value of scientific research?"

"Mom and Dad took it to the shop," Kevin told Giles. "They're trying to get someone to turn it back into a film projector."

"Not a chance," muttered Tina. "They don't

know what they're dealing with."

"Hey, I think I've got it," said Kevin. "Tina, look at this. I take these two dice and put them in my hand." Kevin made a fist, hiding the dice. "Now I say the magic words — "

Kevin muttered something under his breath and made a number of dramatic flourishes with his clenched fist.

"And I open my hand and — "

"They're still right there," said Tina blandly, pointing at the dice in Kevin's palm.

"What? Hey, no fair!" cried Kevin. "It worked last time. You must put a jinx on me. You take away all my confidence!"

Suddenly it all clicked in Giles's head.

"That's it!" he cried.

"What?" said Kevin.

"That's why Mr. Kapoor can't come back!"

"Someone put a jinx on him?" Kevin asked.

"No, no!" exclaimed Giles, jumping up. "Because he's lost all his confidence!"

"Explain yourself more fully, Barnes," Tina requested in a calm voice.

"The problem isn't the magic!" Giles went on excitedly. "How can Mr. Kapoor possibly come back if he thinks he's a terrible magician! He doesn't want to come back! He wants to stay invisible!"

Kevin nodded slowly. "There are times I've wanted to be invisible," he admitted.

"There are times I've wanted to *make* you invisible," Tina admitted.

"I think I know how to bring him back," said Giles.

"How?" Kevin asked.

"It's just an idea," said Giles. "I'll need to think it out first."

* * *

"You're going to have a magic show," said Giles.

"What on earth are you talking about!" exclaimed Mr. Kapoor. "I'm invisible!"

"You're going to reappear and give a magic show," Giles told him.

"Oh no I'm not! The last magic show I gave was a disaster! I wouldn't do another one for a million dollars!"

"Well," said Giles, "I'm afraid it's a little late. I've already arranged it with Miss Hibbins. She's agreed to let us have the show in the library next week."

"But this is crazy!" cried Mr. Kapoor. "How am

I going to reappear? With the energy ray?"

"I wouldn't recommend it," Kevin said. "Not unless you want to end up looking like a sizzled shoe."

"I've discovered a very powerful magic," said Giles mysteriously.

"You have?" said Mr. Kapoor.

"You have?" echoed Kevin.

"Yes," said Giles. "I have. And by the day of the magic show, you'll be ready to reappear, Mr. Kapoor."

"You seem awfully sure," said the invisible magician.

"It's never failed yet," said Giles. "Not on anyone. So do you agree to have the show?"

"All right, yes."

"There's one other thing," said Giles.

"What?"

"I'd like to be your assistant. That is, if you think I'd be any help," he added humbly. "I've been practising every day."

"I've never had an assistant," mused Mr. Kapoor. "Usually only the very best have assistants. I must say I like the sound of it. I do like the sound of it!"

"Great!" said Giles. "We'll make posters, and put them up around the library and the classrooms at school!"

"We'll spread the word!" added Kevin.

"We can practice every day after school," said Mr. Kapoor. "Let's start right away!"

Chapter 11

The Great Kapoor

"YOU LOOK LIKE you ran away from the circus," Tina said.

"It's my costume!" said Giles indignantly.

"She's just jealous," Kevin told him.

It was the day of the big magic show, and the three of them were waiting in the library for Mr. Kapoor. Giles peeked through the curtain. Miss Hibbins was rushing around, making last minute preparations. She had done a fantastic job. She had rigged up a curtain across one end of the large reading room, and had arranged semi-circular rows of chairs for the audience. Black and orange streamers dipped from shelf to shelf, and multi-coloured balloons bobbed up against the ceiling.

Already people were starting to arrive and take their seats.

"Where is he?" said Giles worriedly. "He's going to be late."

"I'm here," said a nervous voice beside him. "Listen, Barnes, I don't think I can do this. I'm no good!"

"Of course, you're good!" said Giles. "You're better than good! You're terrific!"

"You're The Great Kapoor!" said Kevin. "Don't forget that."

"Sure, but what about this powerful magic you promised," said the invisible magician. "It's going to make me reappear, right?"

"Well, it doesn't work quite like that," said Giles. "I'll read out the words, and they'll give you the power to reappear yourself! Are you ready?"

"I hope this works," came the magician's uncertain voice.

Giles cleared his throat.

"Tangent. Cosine. Algorithmic!"

"Oh, I like the sound of this," said Mr. Kapoor.

"Convex. Vector. Parabolic!" said Giles.

"Wonderful!" said the magician. "I feel better already!"

"Tetra. Octo. Trapezoidal! Rhomboid. Ellipse. Hexahedral!"

"Yes, yes, I can feel the magic in that one!"

Giles could see that Tina was about to say something, but he shot her a look that changed her mind.

"Now all you have to do is reappear when I give the signal," Giles told the magician. "You're going to be fantastic!"

"Do you really think so?"

"I know it," said Giles confidently.

Miss Hibbins poked her head behind the curtain.

"Everything ready?" she asked.

Giles nodded.

"Is the invisible man here?" she inquired.

"I'm here," said Mr. Kapoor.

"Thrilling," she gasped. "Just thrilling!"

The curtains drew back and Giles walked nervously out in front of the audience. There was quite a crowd — lots of kids from school, and plenty of parents, too. Kevin and Tina were just taking their seats at the front, and Kevin gave him the thumbs-up sign. He couldn't find his father, but he knew he was there, watching.

"Ladies and gentleman!" Giles said, in as big a voice as possible. "I'm pleased to introduce . . . The Great Kapoor!"

He swept his arm through the air to where Mr. Kapoor was supposed to appear.

But there was nothing to be seen.

"The Great Kapoor!" Giles said again. What if Mr. Kapoor had run away! What if he'd chickened out! What if his powerful magic hadn't been good enough!

But then there was a burst of smoke, and the crackling and twinkling of a hundred firecrackers.

Giles gaped in amazement.

The smoke cleared.

And there he was. The Great Kapoor!

The audience applauded madly.

He wasn't at all the way Giles had imagined him. He imagined someone taller and fatter. He imagined someone with a bushy beard and a big chest. As it was, you couldn't have said Mr. Kapoor was an impressive man. He was quite small and thin, and he would have been very ordinary looking without his high black top hat, his flowing purple cape, and his gleaming black magician's uniform with gold piping.

Giles thought he looked magnificent.

The applause was just beginning to die down.

The Great Kapoor started off slowly with the billiard ball trick. Then he picked up the pace. He did the bottomless jar trick, he did the floating hoops. With Giles's help, he did the Mongolian juggling trick, the turtle into the hare, and then the extravagant flaming zucchini! The Great Kapoor was fabulous!

The audience applauded furiously.

"And now," said The Great Kapoor, "for the grand finale, I will perform the Disappearing Act. I will need a volunteer from the audience."

A hush fell over the crowd.

"Perhaps you would like to volunteer, young lady," said Mr. Kapoor, pointing at Tina Quark.

"Me?" said Tina. Giles thought she looked a little pale.

"There's nothing to be afraid of, my dear. Come right up."

Tina walked hesitantly to the front.

"Are you sure you're up to this?" Giles whispered to the magician.

"Never felt better," The Great Kapoor whispered back.

"Observe!" he cried out to the audience. He swirled a large blanket around Tina, and when he pulled it away, she had disappeared into thin air.

The crowd gasped in amazement.

"And now," cried The Great Kapoor, swirling out the blanket for a second time, "she re-appears!"

There was a flash of light, and Tina was back again, looking slightly bewildered.

With a colossal burst of cheering, the magic show was over. Fans flocked to the front to ask The Great Kapoor to sign autographs. Giles saw his father making his way through the crowd towards him.

"It was a fabulous show," said Mr. Barnes, giving Giles a hug. "And you were great."

"Thanks," said Giles.

"You've made this library a much more exciting place!" exclaimed Miss Hibbins. "I think we'll have a magic show every week!"

"You've got to teach me some of those tricks!" said Kevin.

Tina still seemed a little dazed. She kept looking at her arms and legs, making sure they were still attached to the rest of her body.

"I have to admit, Barnes," she began, "your methods are highly unscientific, but you seem to have found the answer to a very difficult problem."

"He certainly did!" said The Great Kapoor. "Without Barnes, I'd still be invisible! Now tell me, where did you find such powerful magic?"

"It wasn't magic at all," Giles confessed. "I made it all up."

"You what?" said The Great Kapoor in amazement.

"Yep. It was all gobbledygook from one of my Mom's math textbooks. You reappeared all by yourself."

"But I could feel the magical power inside me!" objected the Great Kapoor. "It was like bottled thunder and lightning!"

"Nope," said Giles. "It was just you. All you."

"Well, if you say so," said the magician. He didn't seem totally convinced, but he looked pleased nonetheless. "All the same, I'd like to give you something in return."

"More magic lessons," said Giles and Kevin instantly.

"Done!" said the Great Kapoor.

"And I was wondering," whispered Kevin, "do you think you could teach me how to do that disappearing thing with Tina?"

Kenneth Oppel's first book, *Colin's Fantastic Video Adventure,* was published when he was fifteen years old. Since then he has written sixteen more books, including the best-selling novels *Silverwing* and *Sunwing,* both of which have won the Canadian Library Association's Book of the Year for Children Award.

Ken lives in Toronto with his wife and two children. Visit his website at: *http://members.aol.com/kenoppel/*